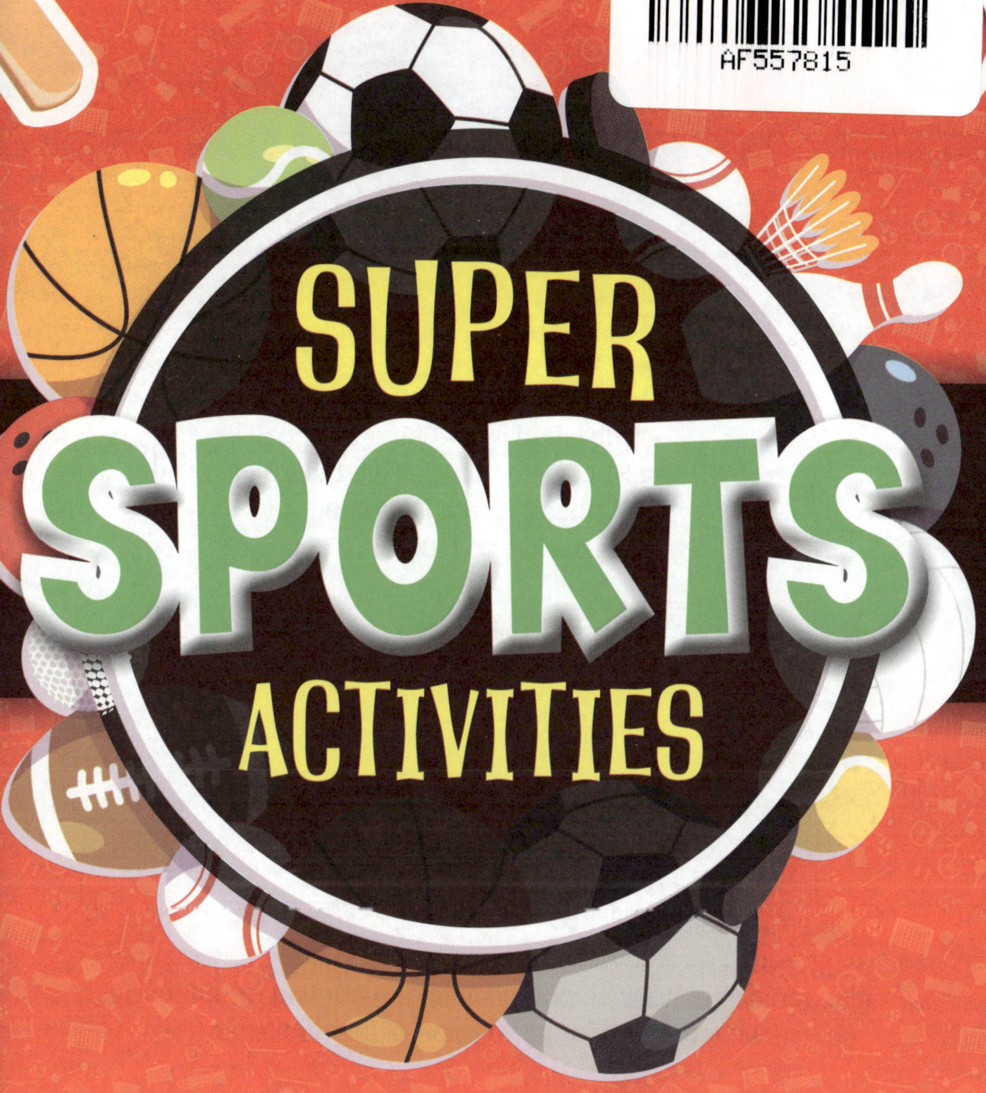

SUPER SPORTS ACTIVITIES

Published in Moonstone
by Rupa Publications India Pvt. Ltd 2024
7/16, Ansari Road, Daryaganj
New Delhi 110002

Sales centres:
Bengaluru Chennai
Hyderabad Jaipur Kathmandu
Kolkata Mumbai Prayagraj

P-ISBN: 978-93-90260-82-9
E-ISBN: 978-93-90260-66-9

First impression 2024

10 9 8 7 6 5 4 3 2 1

Printed in India

Match the multiplication problems to their answers.

4 X 2

3 X 5

5 X 2

2 X 3

Match the players with their answer footballs.

Cross out the extra flying footballs so that the total matches with the number given.

Count the number of each shape on the trophy and write the answer in the boxes.

Take the player through the problems whose sums are 10 and help him reach the net.

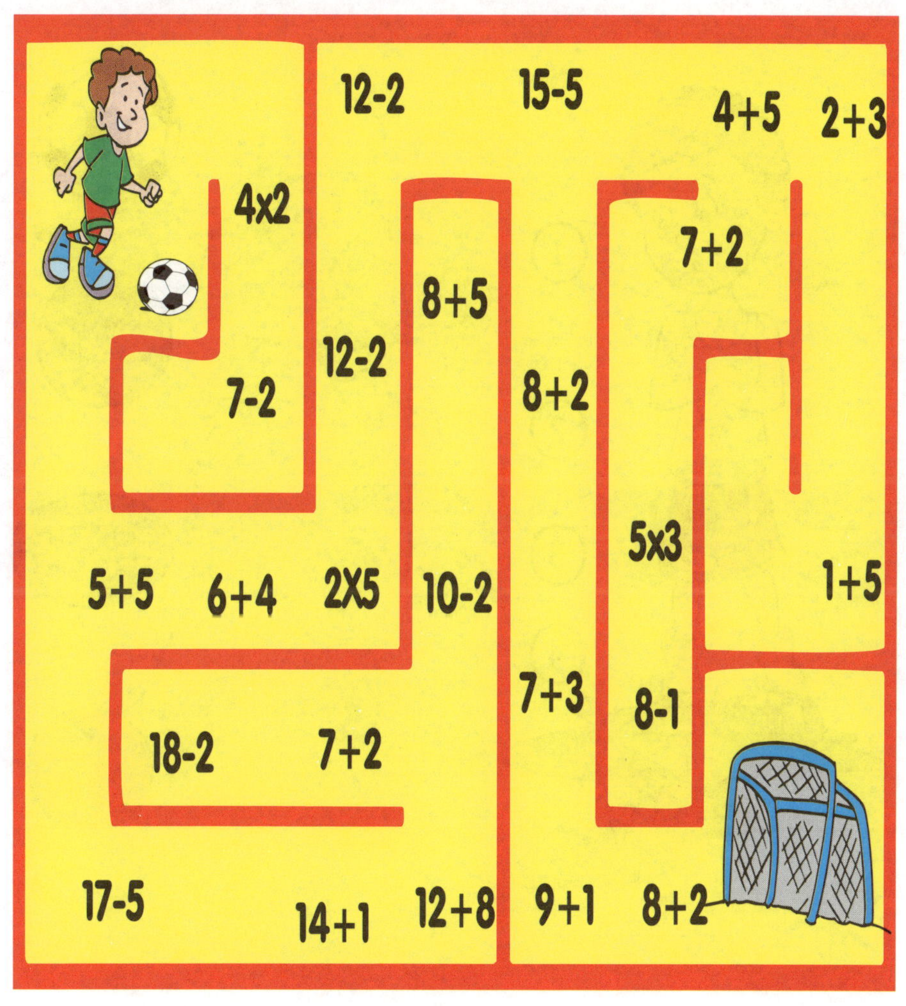

Alex has lost his basketball. Can you identify and circle his basketball?

Which part has been cut from the picture? Tick the correct circle.

John has to throw the ball into the net. Help him reach the net through the maze.

Circle the shadow that is the exact copy of the colourful picture.

Spot the odd one out.

Jenny loves to play with his basketball. Complete the picture by joining the dots and numbers together.

A group of boys are playing basketball. Find the differences between the two pictures.

Consult the picture graph, and write the answers for the given questions.

★ How many  are there? ____

★ How many  are there? ____

★ How many  are there? ____

★ How many  are there? ____

★ Are there more  than ?

Match the pictures with the numbers.

Add or subtract to get 25 as the answer.

Calculate the sums and write the answers in the empty circles. Colour all the even numbers with yellow and the odd numbers with green.

Complete the mathematical problems, using the codes.

= 4 = 8 = 9 = 7

+ =

− =

+ =

- =

Number the picture pieces in the correct order.

Circle the basketballs whose answers are 25.

Fill in the missing numbers in the basketballs given below. Hint: Recount the timetable of 3.

Number the pictures from the smallest to the biggest.

Go through the route (mathematical problems) whose answers are 10 and find John's basketball.

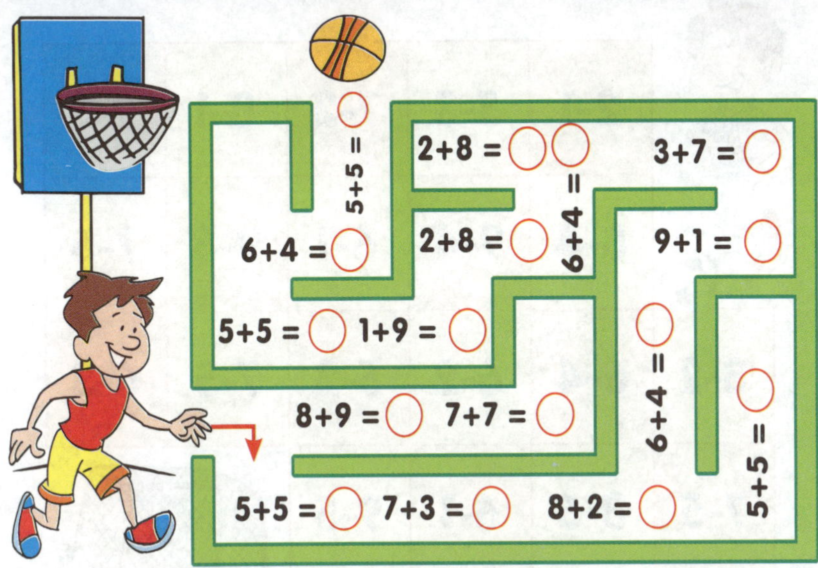

Look carefully at the picture. Fill in the correct letter in the missing part.

Ⓐ Ⓑ Ⓒ Ⓓ

Colour the boxes that show a difference of 4 to find a path to the net.

	2-1	5-3	7-2	8-1	9-3
	8-4	9-4	6-1	9-8	7-6
3-2	6-4	6-2	5-2	7-5	6-3
7-5	8-6	6-1	9-5		

Subtract the numbers and help the players reach the last ball.

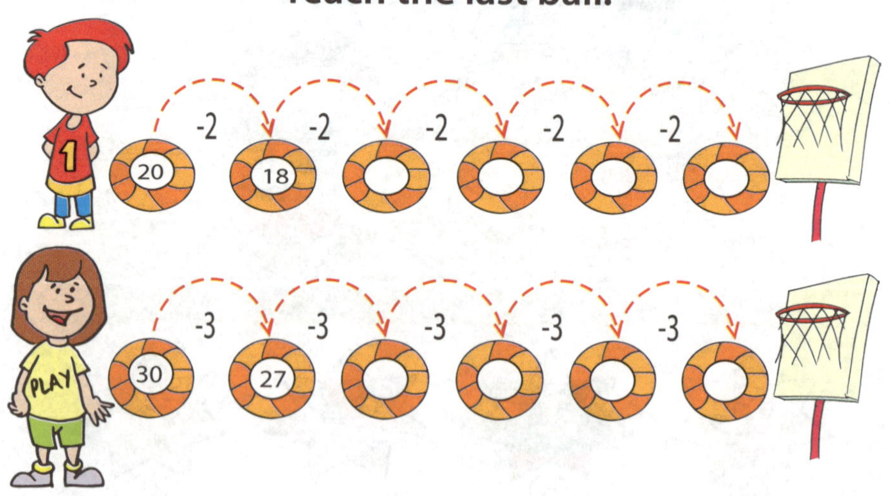

Colour the basketball player.

Find the missing puzzle letter.

Circle the number that equals to the number of balls in the picture.

Look at the picture below and copy and draw it in the grid.

Count the total number of nets and write it in the circle below.

Follow the dots and complete the activity.

Sam has to go to play basketball in the playground. Arrange the pictures in the proper sequence.

Which is the correct shadow of the boy?

Look at the colourful codes to add bright shades to the picture.

Add the pictures and numbers together in each row to find the total.

+ 8 =

+ 5 =

+ 2 =

Spot the differences between the pictures.

Draw a line from each basketball to its respective answer on the net.

Can you help Alex put the basketball inside the net?

Complete the picture of the boy playing basketball. Colour it, too.

Follow the dots and complete the picture. Colour it brightly.

Use the codes given in the box to colour the picture.

Bring John to his basketball.

Add up the objects and tick the correct number.

15 14 17

Add up the objects and tick the correct number.

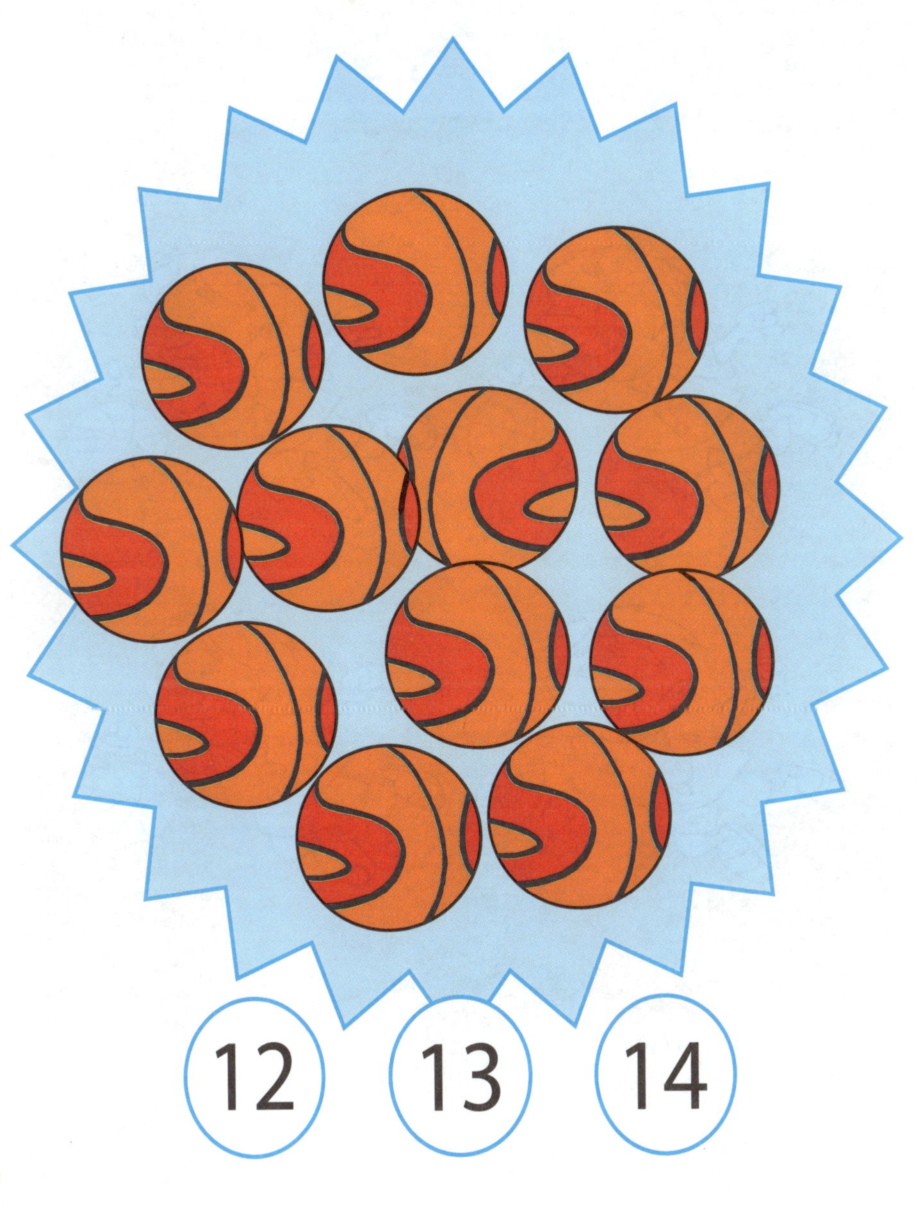

Colour any 2 basketball players.

Tick on the boy's appropriate shadow.

Use bright colours to shade the picture.

Put in the correct numbers in the magic square.

5	+		=	15
+		+		-
15	-	5	=	
=		=		=
20	-		=	5

Trace and colour the picture beautifully.

Look at the number line and fill in the correct numbers. Write the answers in the space provided.

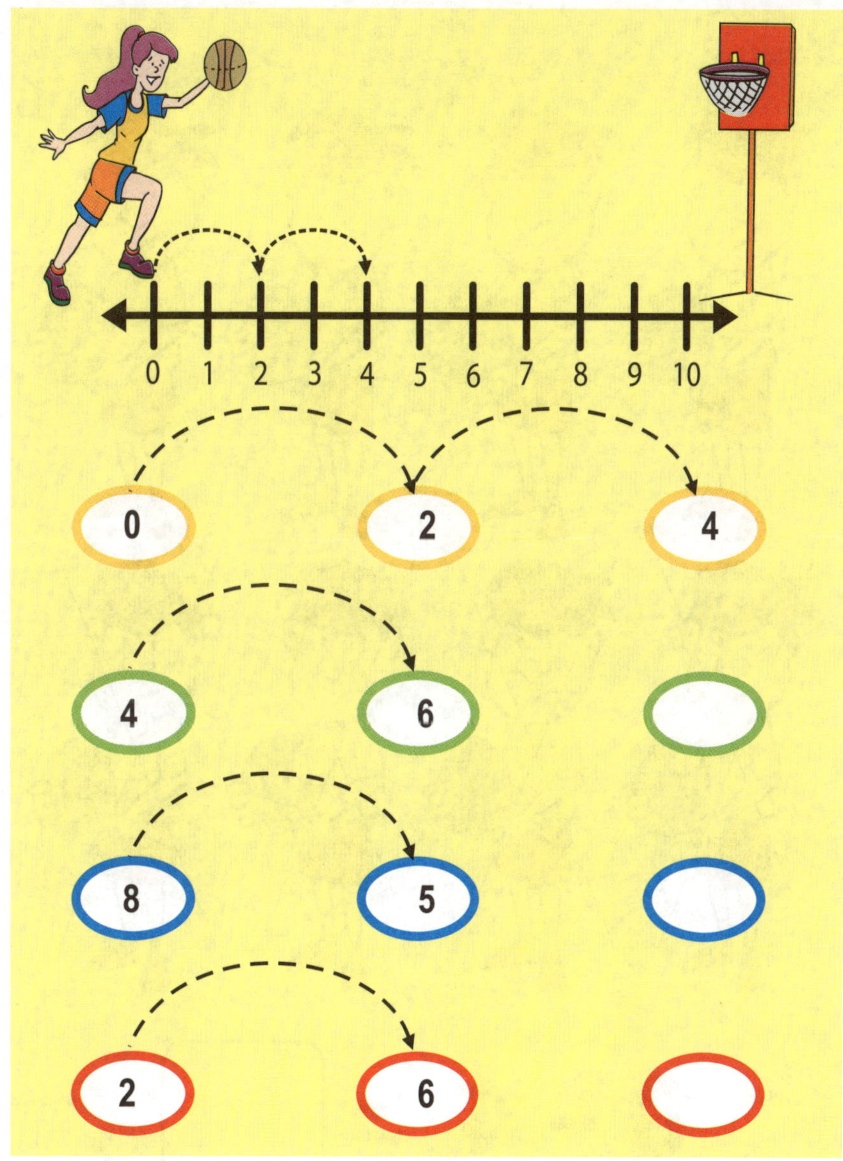

Count, subtract and write the answer.

8 – 4 = ☐

Take each player to its respective ball. Mark the route with the pencil.

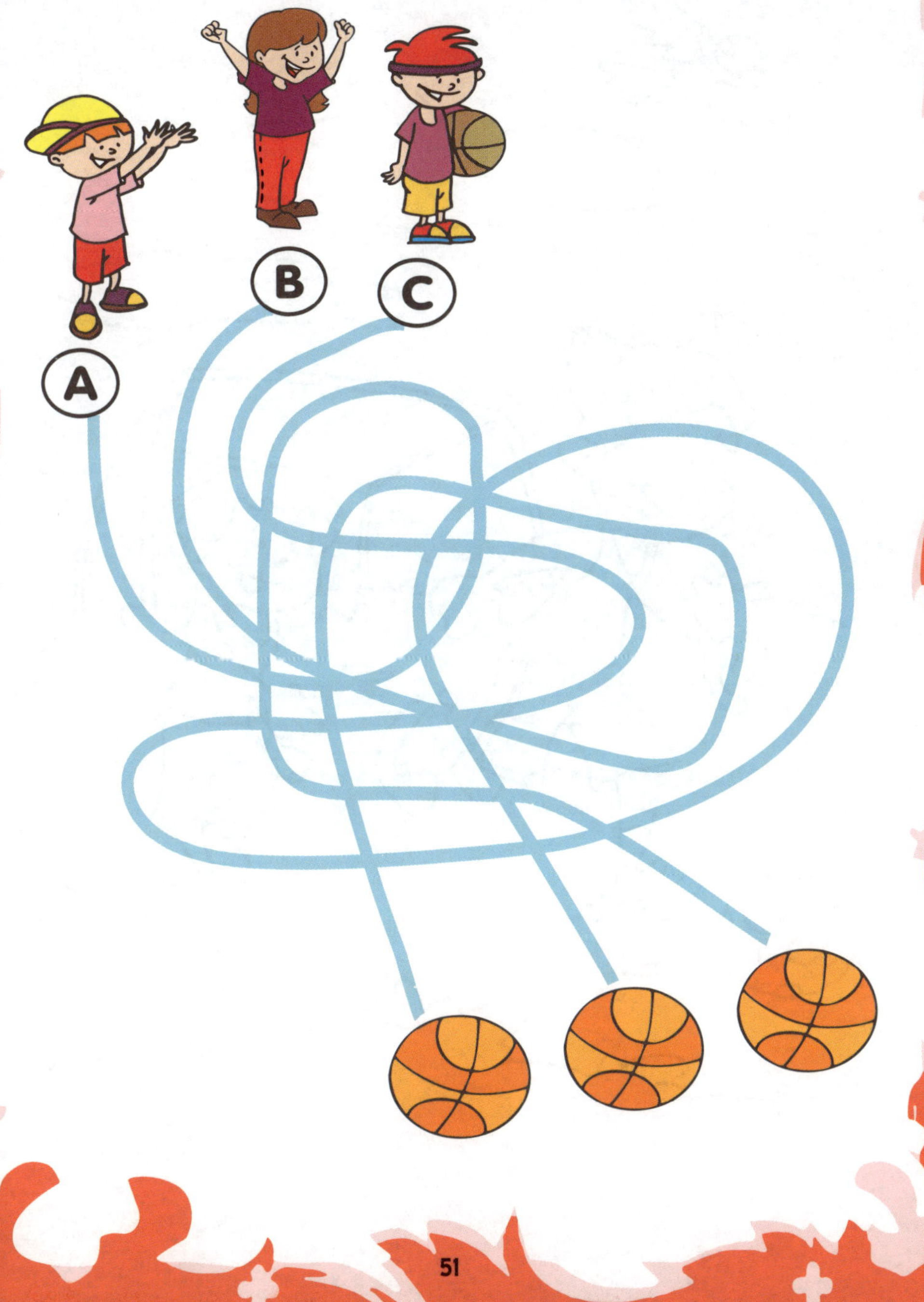

Colour the picture brightly.

Colour the black and white picture brightly.

Write the missing letter from the picture.

Colour any two players to make 15.

Write three different addition equations whose answers are 20.

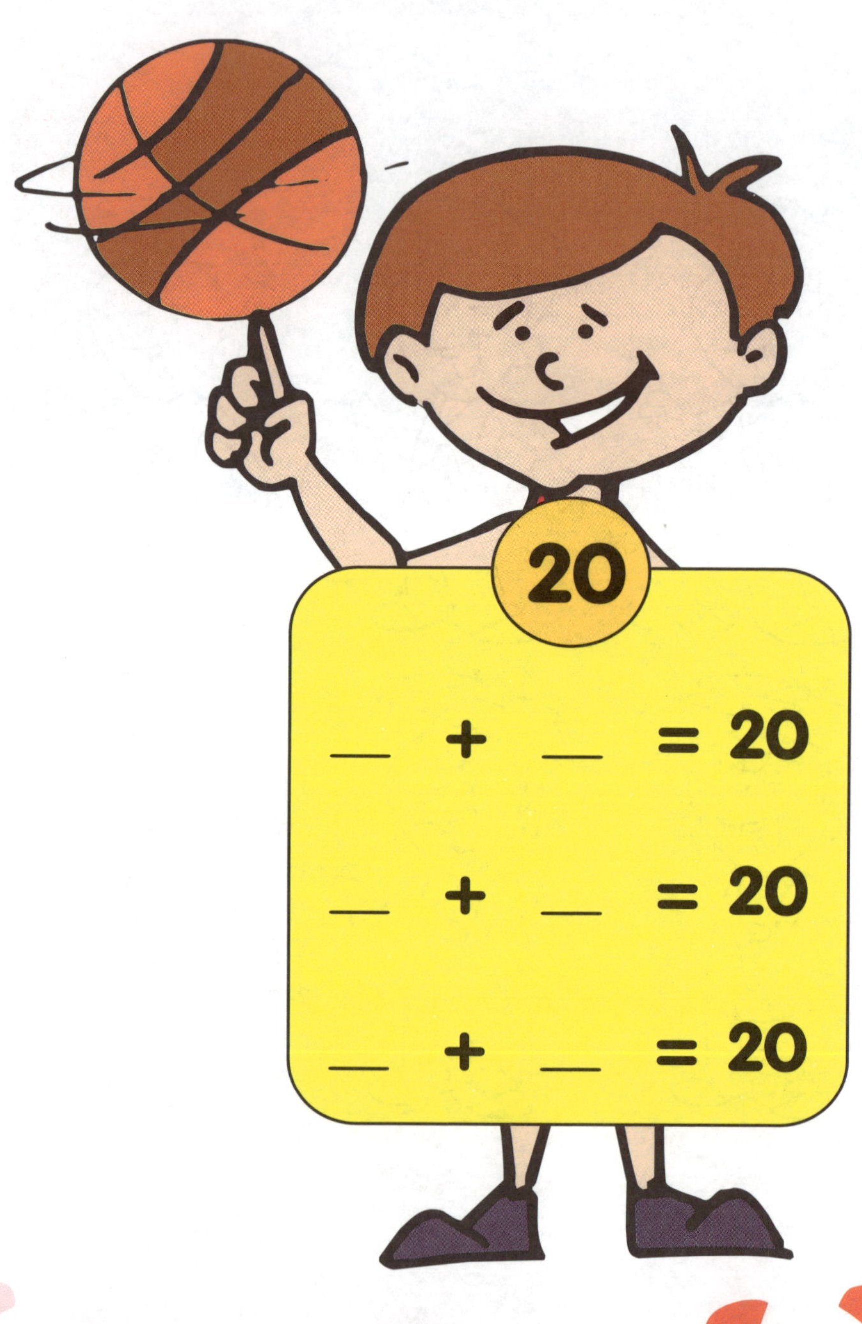

Copy the picture in the grid and colour it as the picture given.

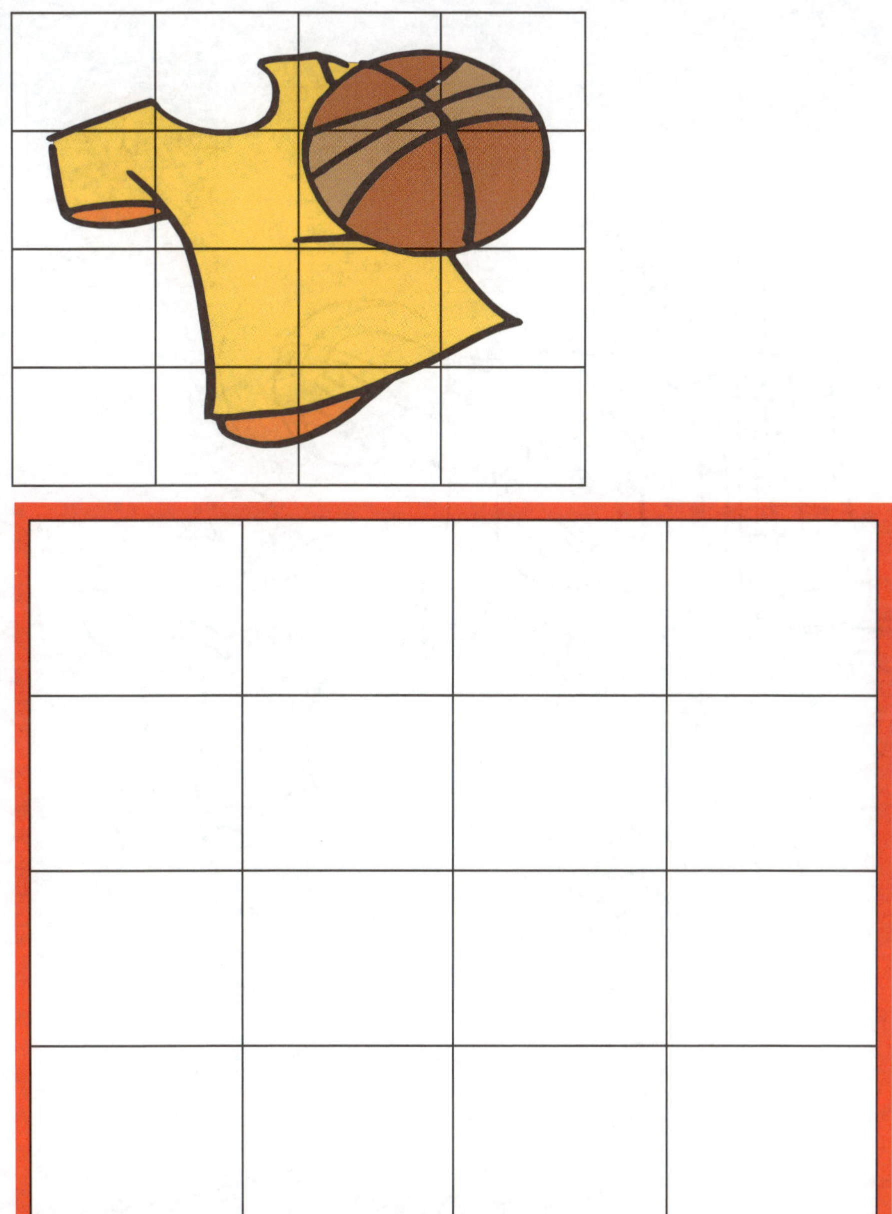

Colour the picture brightly with the crayons.

Trace and colour the picture brightly.

Count the basketballs and cross out seven of them. Then find the answer.

16-7 =

Can you create a route for the girl and assist her in reaching the other end?

Can you spot the differences between the pictures?

How many basketball post are there?
Tick the correct number.

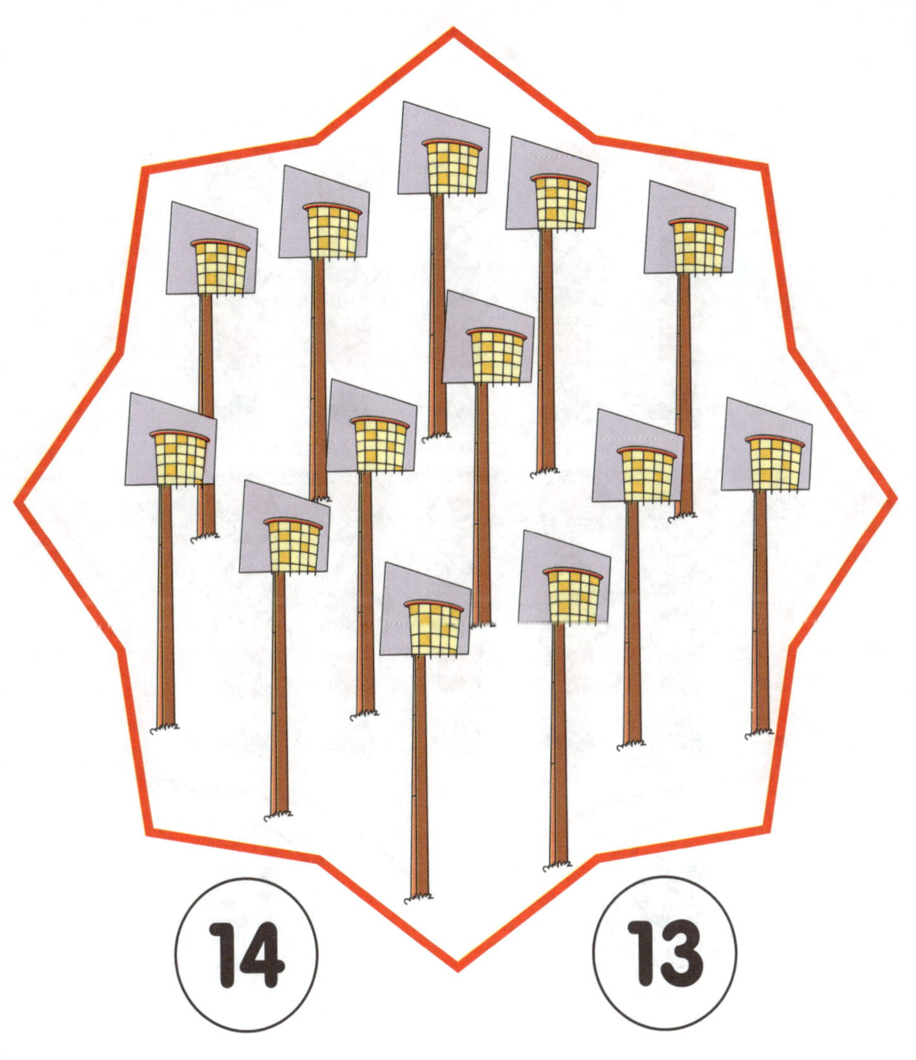

How many boys are there?
Tick the correct number.

10

12

Draw a boy, as shown, in the blank grid.
Colour it, too.

Follow the dots and numbers correctly and join them. Colour the boy.

Colour any two players that sum up to 15.

Help the boy reach the basketball court.

Complete the picture by ticking the missing part?

A

B

C

D

Colour the basketball player with different colours using the codes.

1	2	3	4	5	6	7	8	9

Match the faces with their respective bodies, by placing the correct letters.

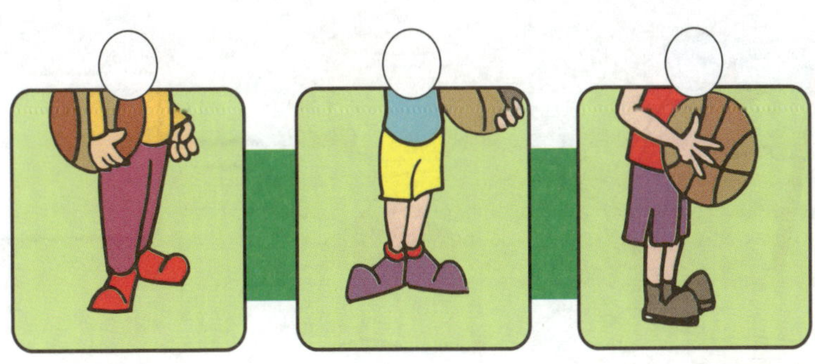

Decode the pictures and find the answers.

Calculate the sums.

5 x 5 = ☐

2 x 5 = ☐

4 x 4 = ☐

7 x 8 = ☐

7 x 2 = ☐

Put the pictures in their proper sequence.

Colour the picture brightly.

Write the numbers that come before and after.

Multiply and find the answers.

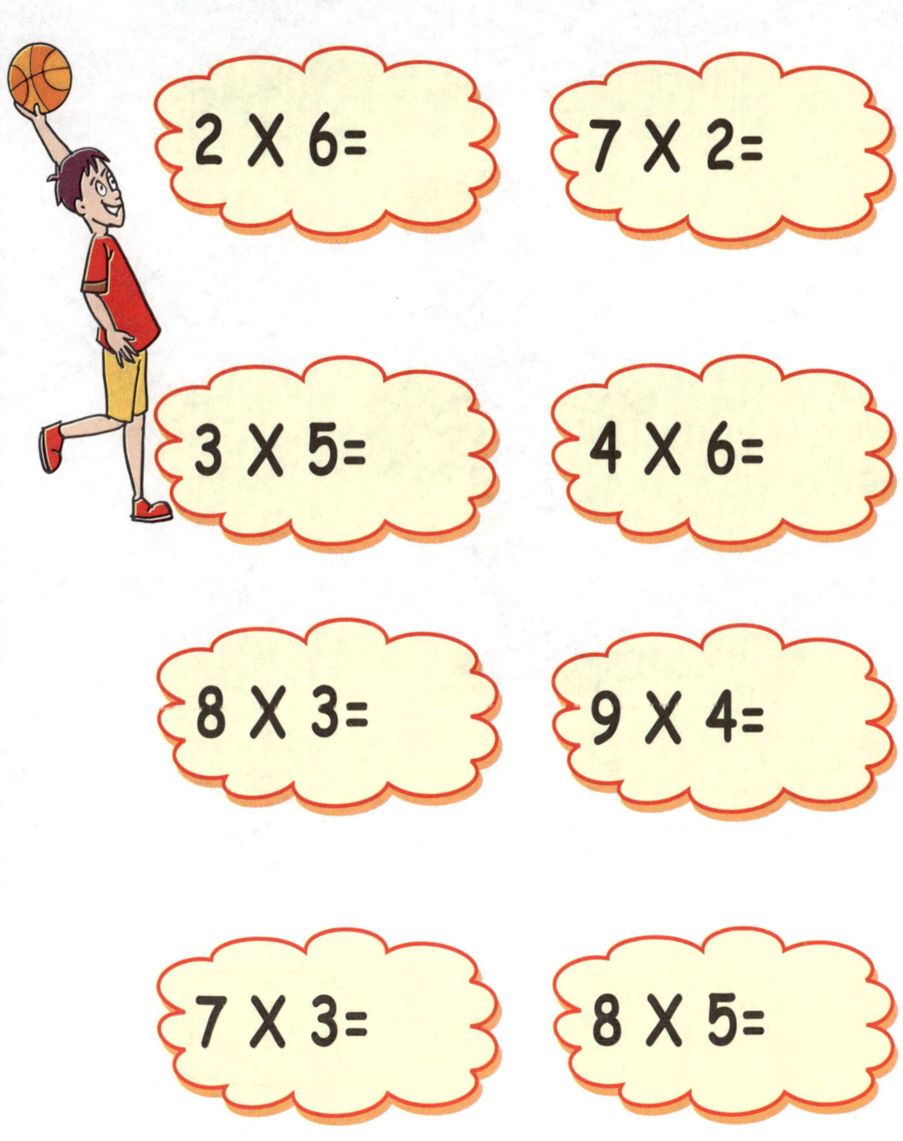

2 X 6=

7 X 2=

3 X 5=

4 X 6=

8 X 3=

9 X 4=

7 X 3=

8 X 5=

Help Jerry count the number of basketballs.
Clue: Before counting, shade the pictures.

Draw the ball, as shown, in the blank grid. Colour it too.

Find the answers of the mathematical problems.

$5 \times 1 =$ ☐

$7 \times 3 =$ ☐

$4 \times 4 =$ ☐

$6 \times 3 =$ ☐

$8 \times 5 =$ ☐

Colour the picture that is of the same size.

Colour the boxes in red colour that show a sum of 16 and help the player reach his friend.

	15 + 1	10 + 6	18 + 6
10 + 10	10 + 6	12 + 4	21 + 6
9 + 4	8 + 8	13 + 3	13 + 6
3 + 1	12 + 4	9 + 5	14 + 12
5 + 6	14 + 2	7 + 9	

Colour the picture brightly.

Add the numbers and find the total.

3 + 3 + 3 + 3 + 3 + 3 = ◯

4 + 4 + 4 + 4 + 4 + 4 = ◯

5 + 5 + 5 + 5 + 5 + 5 = ◯

Find the differences between the pictures.

Draw a boy, as shown, in the blank grid. Colour it, too.

Colour the bigger picture alike the smaller picture.

Fill in the missing numbers in the puzzle.

Complete the picture by ticking the missing triangle.

A

B

C

D

Let's have equal number of balls and nets in the boxes. Think, how?

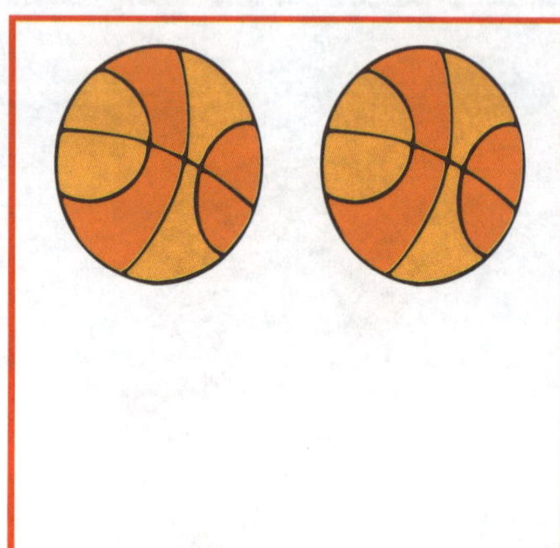

Match with the correct shadow.

Help the boy throw the ball into the net.

Count the total number of boys in the box and tick the correct answer.

6 8

Find the correct shadow of the boy.

Place the pictures in the correct order.

Let's make the picture look colourful.